This Little Tiger book belongs to:

_____

_____

_____

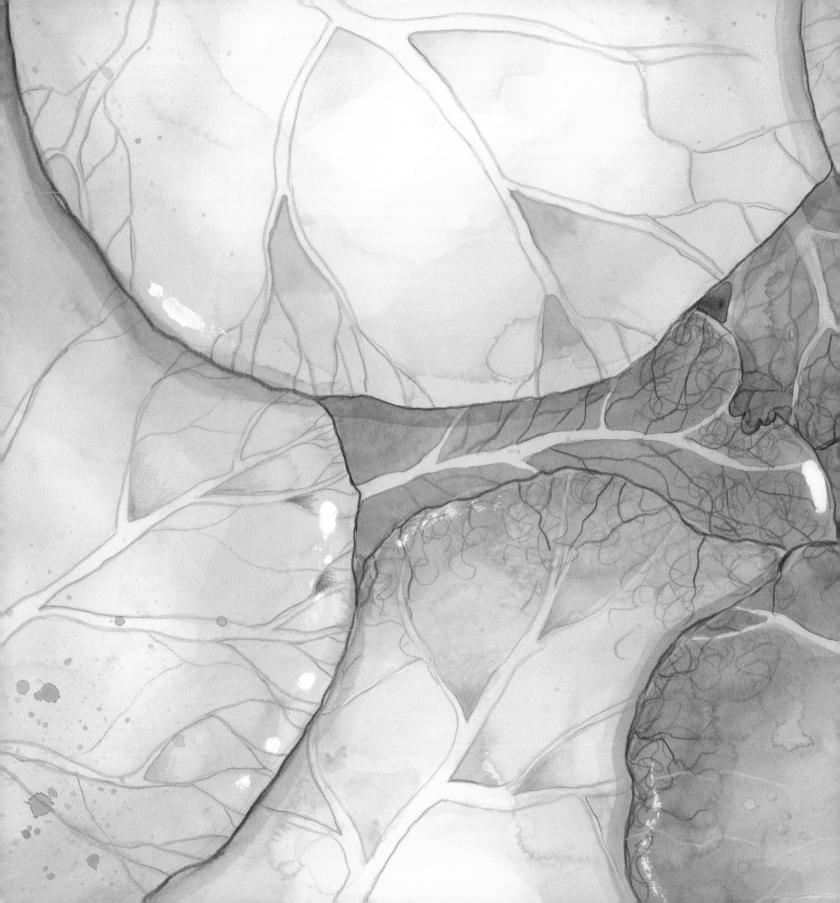

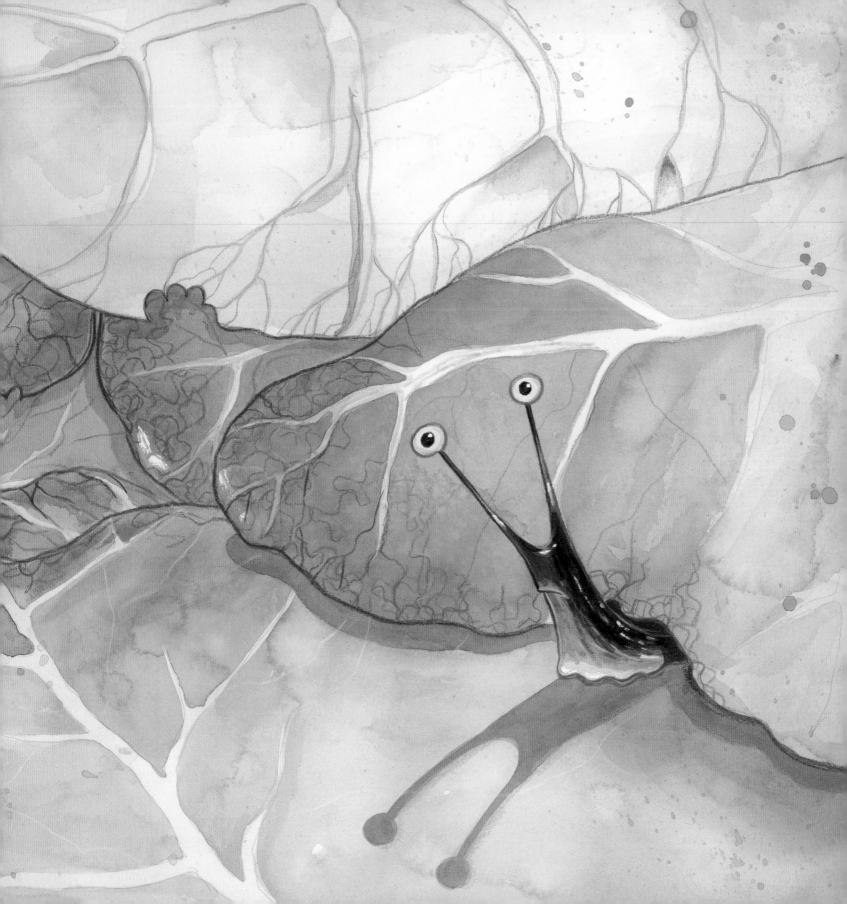

For Kimmy and Copper
~A P

For Eugene
~D R

LITTLE TIGER PRESS LTD,
an imprint of the Little Tiger Group
1 Coda Studios, 189 Munster Road,
London SW6 6AW
www.littletiger.co.uk

First published in Great Britain 2005
This edition published 2017

Don't Say That, Willy Nilly!

by Anna Powell

Illustrated by
David Roberts

LiTTLE TiGER
LONDON

"Willy Nilly," said his mother,
"would you like to go to the shop
and buy some cabbage for dinner?"
"YUK!" said Willy Nilly.

"Don't say that, Willy Nilly," said his mother. "Say, 'YUM, YUM, WHAT A LOVELY DINNER!'"

"Yum, yum, what a lovely dinner?" repeated Willy Nilly.

"That's right," said his mother.

"GOT IT!" said Willy Nilly.

So Willy Nilly set off to the shop.

"YUM, YUM, WHAT A LOVELY DINNER!
YUM, YUM, WHAT A LOVELY DINNER!"
repeated Willy Nilly.

Outside, the men were emptying dustbins.
Willy Nilly said, "Yum, yum,
what a lovely dinner!"

"Don't say that, Willy Nilly," said the dustbin men. "Say, 'GOOD RIDDANCE TO BAD RUBBISH!'"

"Good riddance to bad rubbish?" said Willy Nilly.

"That's right," said the men.

"GOT IT!" said Willy Nilly.

"GOOD RIDDANCE TO BAD RUBBISH! GOOD RIDDANCE TO BAD RUBBISH!"

In the road there was a big removal van.
The neighbours were moving away.
Willy Nilly said, "Good riddance to bad rubbish!"

"Don't say that, Willy Nilly," said Mrs Jiggs. "Say,
'ENJOY YOUR NEW HOME!'"
"Enjoy your new home?" said Willy Nilly.
"That's right," said Mrs Jiggs.
"GOT IT!" said Willy Nilly.

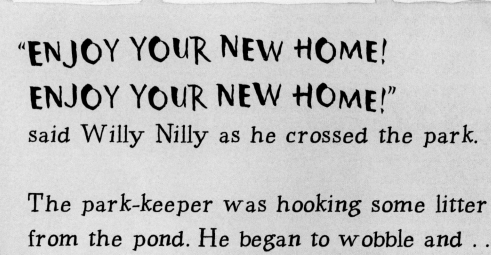

**"ENJOY YOUR NEW HOME!
ENJOY YOUR NEW HOME!"**
said Willy Nilly as he crossed the park.

The park-keeper was hooking some litter
from the pond. He began to wobble and . . .

"Enjoy your new home," said Willy Nilly.

"Don't say that, Willy Nilly," said the park-keeper. "Say, 'CAN I HELP YOU OUT OF THERE?'"

"Can I help you out of there?" said Willy Nilly.

"That's right," said the park-keeper.

"GOT IT!" said Willy Nilly.

Mr Totty's window was open. The parrot
looked at Willy Nilly with a beady yellow eye.
"Can I help you out of there?" said Willy Nilly.
"WATCH OUT, I MIGHT BITE!" said the parrot.

"Watch out, I might bite!"
said Willy Nilly.
  "WATCH OUT, I MIGHT BITE!"
said the parrot.
  "GOT IT!" said Willy Nilly.

"WATCH OUT, I MIGHT BITE!
WATCH OUT, I MIGHT BITE!"

On the pavement Willy met Granny Macaroon.
"Good morning, Willy Nilly!" said Granny Macaroon.
"Watch out, I might bite!" said Willy Nilly.

"Don't say that, Willy Nilly," said Granny Macaroon. "Say, **'WHAT A LOVELY DAY!'"**

"What a lovely day?" said Willy Nilly.

"That's right," said Granny Macaroon.

"**GOT IT!**" said Willy Nilly.

"WHAT A LOVELY DAY! WHAT A LOVELY DAY!"

The window cleaner sped past on his bicycle.

He wasn't looking where he was going.

He was heading straight for the lamp post.

"What a lovely day!" said Willy Nilly.

CRASH!

"Don't say that, Willy Nilly!"
said the window cleaner. "Say,
'HEY, LOOK OUT!'"
"Hey, look out!" repeated Willy Nilly.
"That's right," said the window cleaner.
"GOT IT!" said Willy Nilly.

In the shop, there was a baby in a pram. Willy Nilly saw the baby reach out to a tower of cans. Oh *no*! The cans would fall on top of him.

"HEY, LOOK OUT!" shouted Willy Nilly.

And the baby stopped! Just in time.
"Quick thinking, young man,"
said the shopkeeper. "What can I
do for you?"

"A cabbage, please," said Willy Nilly.
"And what would you like as a thank you?" said the shopkeeper.
Willy Nilly chose his favourite thing – ketchup. "Thank you very much," he said.

Willy Nilly went straight home.

"Did you get the cabbage, Willy Nilly?"
asked his mother.

"GOT IT!" said Willy Nilly.

"Thank you very much,"
said his mother, and
she cooked the cabbage.

Willy Nilly poured ketchup all over his cabbage to make it taste nice.

"YUM, YUM, WHAT A LOVELY DINNER!" said Willy Nilly.

"YUK!" said his mother.

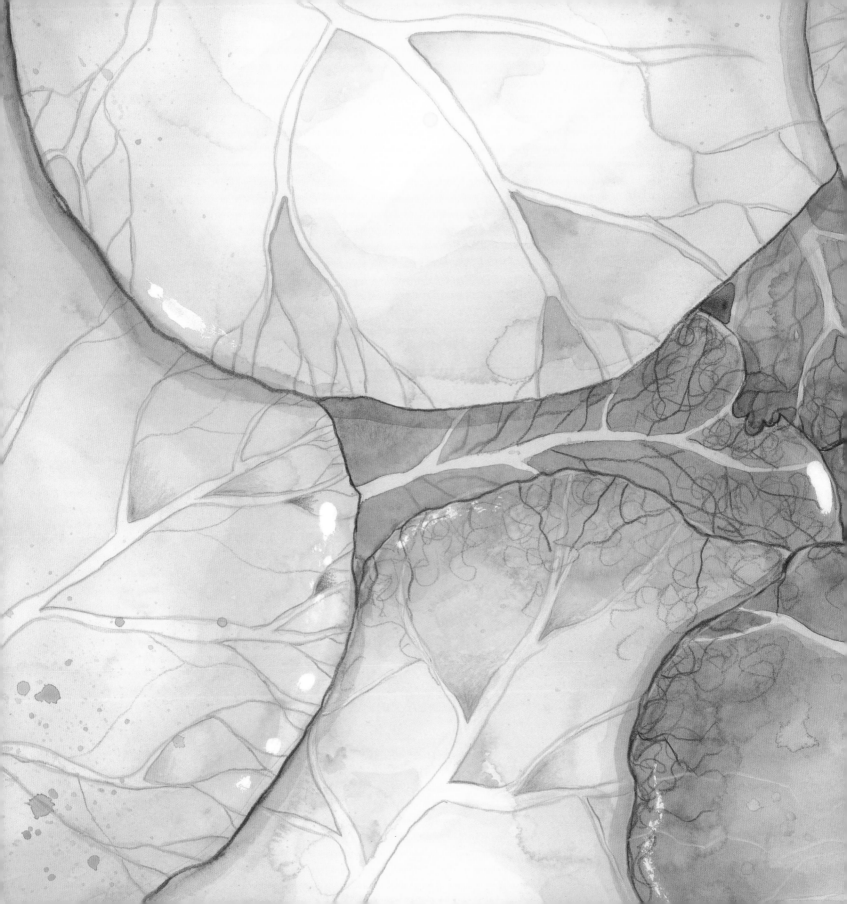

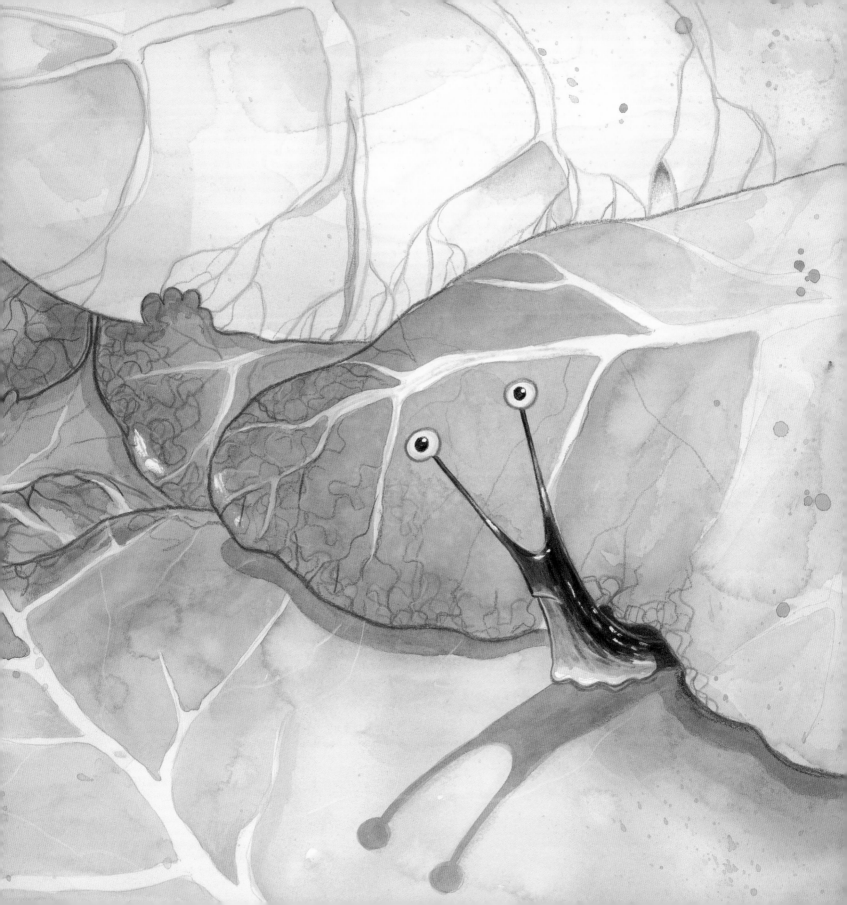